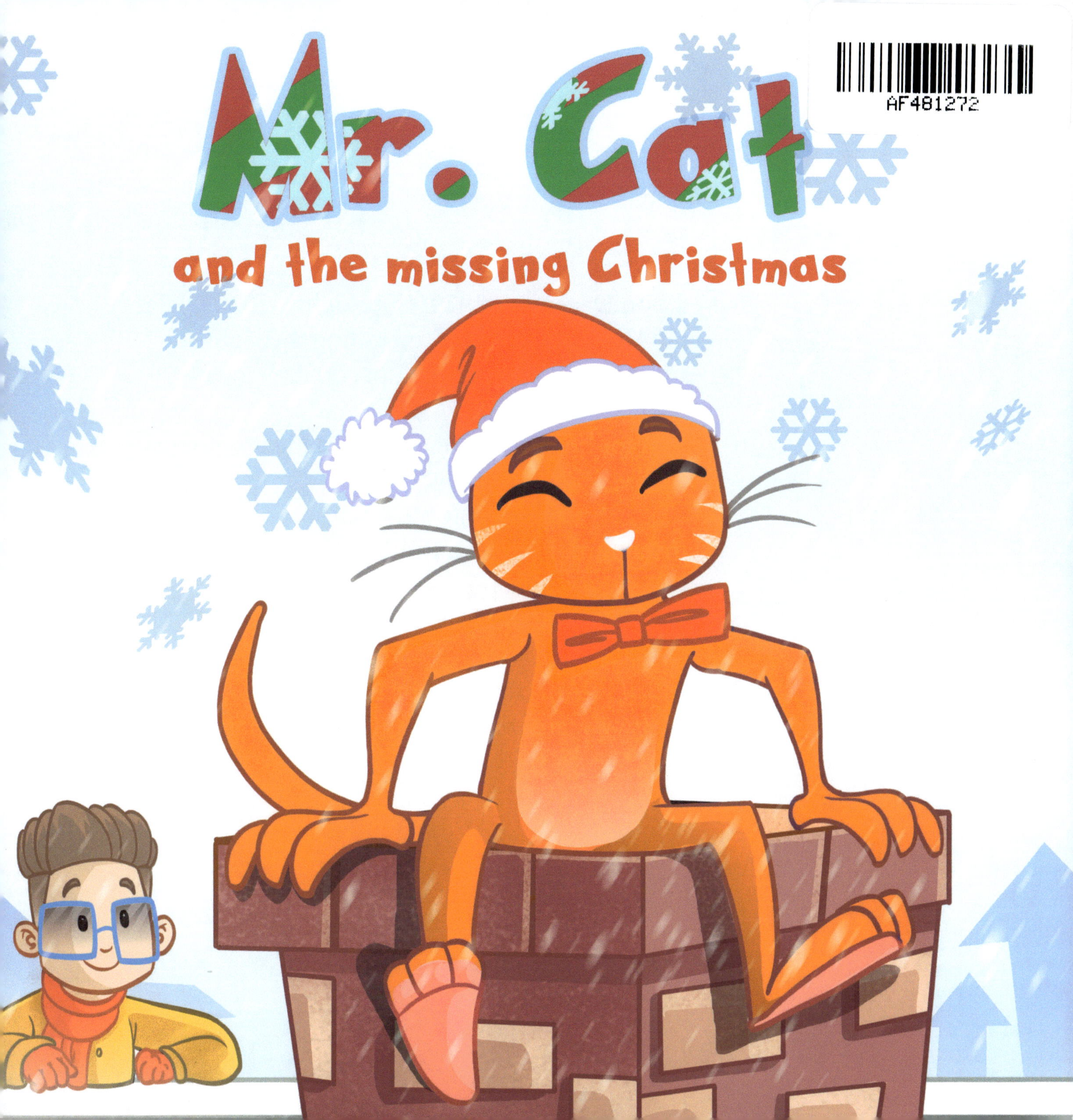

Mr. Cat
and the missing Christmas
AF481272

Thank you for buying our book! We made it with lots of love!
Please follow us on:
Instagram, Pinterest, Facebook,Youtube:
@happytottidxb
Goodreads:@Diala Hanna

Amazon Author Page:
https://www.amazon.com/author/dialahanna

Mr. Cat and Totti go on a fun holiday adventure to find Santa. With only a day left before Christmas morning, will they get to him in time?

On a snowy winter night, Mr. Cat and Totti were sitting on the terrace, all happy and excited, counting one more night till Christmas.

But something was different this time . . . the streets had no decorations!
By this time of year, the whole town is usually filled with lights
and Christmas cheer.

They decided to look for Santa to help save Christmas Eve,
they called the North Pole and asked for Elf Steve.

"Santa is missing!", cried Elf Steve. "We don't know what to do!
Hey, Mr. Cat and Totti, would you help us find him too?"
" Sure", they answered. "We will find him and bring him back to you!"

"Now, where could Santa be? ", Mr. Cat asked Totti.
"We know he likes candy, he must be at the chocolate factory!"

"Look what I have found, chocolate sprinkles on the ground!", Mr. Cat said.
"I bet Santa's hiding behind this giant cookie mound."
Milk

"Oh, no! It can't be! Santa is not here. You have to come and see!", Totti replied. Mr. Cat pointed at the snow and said: "He must have been here because his footprints are clear!"

"Look, another clue!", shouted Mr. Cat. "I can see Santa's shoe. Could he be behind this big tree?"

Finally! There was Santa, sitting on the ground, all sad and angry!

"Hey, Santa! Why are you sad?", Totti asked.

"We have been looking everywhere for you, Christmas is not the same without you!"

"I cannot find Rudolph, my dear", Santa replied. "Christmas cannot be without my best friend, the reindeer."

"Now, where could Rudolph be? We know he likes salad. Let's write him a
message made with carrots and greens!"

Rudolph!
Santa Misses you!

All of a sudden, Rudolph appeared in the sky.
He read the message and landed nearby.

Santa gave Rudolph a big hug. He was so happy to find his best
friend and a big smile replaced his tears.

On Christmas eve, Mr. Cat and Totti stood outside.
They watched Santa and Rudolph distribute gifts all night!

Merry, Merry Christmas!
It's really truly HERE!
We love you Santa! We'll see you next year!

Totti
Mr. Cat
Mr. Cat

# Thank you for buying our book!

We would really appreciate it if you could spare a couple of minutes to write an online review and tell us what you think of it.

Thank you so much
Diala & Antony (A.k.a.Totti)

## Want a free coloring book?

Simply type the address below in your browser:
https://happytottidxb-ec224.gr8.com/

# Interested in our first book?

## The Power of Serious Positive

Perfect bed time story about positivity,
ages 3 to 9

Available on Amazon!

Get it now on the below address:
https://cutt.ly/Ghv5aYZ

www.ingramcontent.com/pod-product-compliance
Lightning Source LLC
Chambersburg PA
CBHW041628110726

48005CB00002B/530